Nate the Great

and the
Missing
Birthday Snake

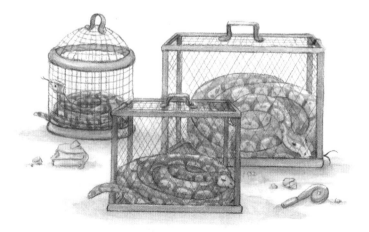

Nate the Great

and the

Missing Birthday Snake

by Andrew Sharmat
and Marjorie Weinman Sharmat

illustrated by Jody Wheeler
in the style of Marc Simont

A YEARLING BOOK

ACKNOWLEDGMENTS

*Jody Wheeler would like to thank the families who helped
Nate the Great on the road: the Phillips family and the Schnur family
on Saratoga Lake, the Fisher family in Laguna, the Spensieri family, and
Satish Kumar, the owner of the Robinhood Motel in Ballston Spa.*

This is a work of fiction. Names, characters, places, and incidents either are the
product of the author's imagination or are used fictitiously. Any resemblance to
actual persons, living or dead, events, or locales is entirely coincidental.

Text copyright © 2017 by Andrew Sharmat and Marjorie Weinman Sharmat
Cover art and interior illustrations copyright © 2017 by Jody Wheeler
Extra Fun Activities copyright © 2018 by Emily Costello
Extra Fun Activities illustrations copyright © 2018 by Jody Wheeler

All rights reserved. Published in the United States by Yearling,
an imprint of Random House Children's Books, a division of Penguin Random
House LLC, New York. Originally published in hardcover in the United States by
Delacorte Press, an imprint of Random House Children's Books, in 2017.

New illustrations of Nate the Great, Sludge, Rosamond,
Annie, Claude, Harry, Fang, and the Hexes by Jody Wheeler
based upon original drawings by Marc Simont.

Yearling and the jumping horse design are registered trademarks of
Penguin Random House LLC.

Visit us on the Web! rhcbooks.com

Educators and librarians, for a variety of teaching tools,
visit us at RHTeachersLibrarians.com

Library of Congress Cataloging-in-Publication Data is available upon request.

ISBN 978-1-101-93467-8 (hardcover) — ISBN 978-1-101-93469-2 (lib. bdg.) —
ISBN 978-1-101-93470-8 (pbk.) — ISBN 978-1-101-93468-5 (ebook)

Printed in the United States of America
10 9 8 7 6 5 4 3 2 1
First Yearling Edition 2018

To Nathan and Madeline
—A.S. and M.W.S.

To cousins Ann, Arlene, Julie, and Anne
—J.W.

Chapter One

An Invitation

My name is Nate the Great.

I am a detective.

I have a dog named Sludge.

He is a detective too.

It was morning.

We were in the kitchen.

I was eating pancakes.

Sludge was chewing on a bone.

We heard scratching noises at the door.

It sounded like a cat scratching.
I opened the door.
I saw Rosamond with her cat Super Hex.
As always, Rosamond looked strange.
So did Super Hex.
Rosamond was pulling a wagon.
Her other cats, Big Hex, Little Hex, and
Plain Hex, were riding inside.
The wagon looked like a birthday cake.
Rosamond looked proud.

"Aren't you going to ask why my cats are
in a wagon that looks like a birthday cake?"
said Rosamond.
I, Nate the Great, was not going to ask.
Because then Rosamond would tell me.
She told me anyway.
"Sunday is my cousin Elizabeth's birthday.
She's visiting. I'm having a party for her
in my backyard.
Here is your invitation."

I looked at the invitation.
There was no writing on it.
Just scratch marks.
"Did one of your cats write the invitation?"
I asked.
"Little Hex did. Super Hex tried,
but he kept ripping up the papers
with his big claws."

That was more than I, Nate the Great,
wanted to know.
"So you'll come?" Rosamond asked.
"When is the party?" I said.
Rosamond pointed to the invitation.
"It says right here. Sunday at two o'clock."
I looked at the invitation.
It didn't say anything.
Unless you knew how to read
cat scratch marks.

"Does your cousin have four cats, like you?"
I asked.

"She has no cats," Rosamond said.

I was glad about that.

"She has four snakes," she said.

"Snakes?"

"Ball pythons, actually."

"Pythons?"

I, Nate the Great, suddenly remembered
that I had many things to do on Sunday.
Many, many things.
I would not have time to attend a birthday
party full of dangerous, slimy snakes.
But I could not explain this to Rosamond.
She and her cats were gone.
They had more invitations to deliver.

Chapter Two
Raining Pythons

Sunday was warm and cloudy.

It looked like it might rain.

I hoped that Rosamond would cancel

her party.

I had no cases to solve.

That meant I had no excuses.

Unless the party was rained out,

I would have to go.

The phone rang.

It was Rosamond.

"I have great news.
The party is going on as planned.
Rain or shine.
I don't want you to worry."
I, Nate the Great,
was worried about a lot of things.
I was worried that the pythons would be large.
I was worried that they would have big fangs.
And be out of their cages.
I was worried that they would be hungry.
And not for birthday cake.

I was *not* worried that the party
would be canceled.
I wrote a note to my mother.

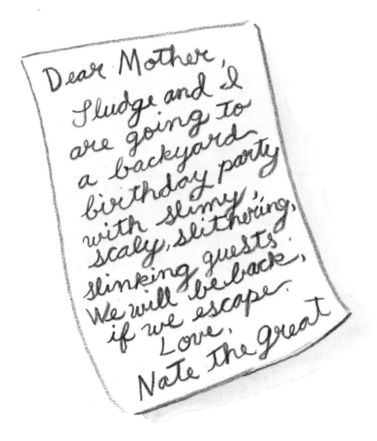

Sludge and I walked to Rosamond's house.
It was raining hard now.
Maybe the party would be canceled after all.
We entered Rosamond's backyard.
Finally some good news.
There was no sign of a party.
I saw only Rosamond and someone
I suspected was her cousin Elizabeth.
And three really big, scary-looking snakes
in three different cages.
"I'm glad you and Sludge could make it
to my cousin's party," said Rosamond.

"Elizabeth, meet Nate the Great."
Elizabeth looked like Rosamond.
She had the same long hair but red.
They had on the same dress,
but hers was white.
Elizabeth also had the same strange look
on her face.
"Call me Lizzy," she said.
"Nate the Great, please meet my pet snakes."
I, Nate the Great, did not want to meet
Lizzy's snakes.
Sludge took a step back.
He did not want to meet Lizzy's snakes.
"This is Super Chomp," Lizzy said.
She pointed to a large snake in a metal cage.
"Then there's Big Chomp, Little Chomp,
and—"
"Plain Chomp?" I said.
"That's a strange name for a snake," Lizzy said.

She pulled out a photograph.
It was a picture of
a snake riding on top
of a car.
The car was big.
The snake was bigger.
"His name is
Ultra-Giant Goliath Chomp.
I call him UGG Chomp for short,"
Lizzy said.
I looked at UGG Chomp.
He wasn't big.
He was ultra-big.

His teeth weren't large.
They were ultra-large.
And he looked hungry.

"Isn't he beautiful?" Lizzy asked.

"Beautiful" was not the word I had in mind.

I changed the subject.

"What is he doing on top of a car?" I asked.

"It's his favorite place," Lizzy said.

"He loves to ride around town."

I did not want to know the answer to my
next question. I asked it anyway.
"Where is UGG Chomp now?"
"We can't find him," Lizzy said.
"When it started to rain,
we moved the party indoors.
We brought all the food inside.
Then we came back to check on the snakes.
The three smaller ones were in their cages."
"Was UGG Chomp in his cage too?"
I asked.

"He doesn't have a cage," Lizzy said.
"We couldn't find one big enough."
"I'm not surprised," I said.
"We're looking for UGG Chomp now,"
Rosamond said.
"Can you help us?"
"I hope no one stole him," Lizzy said.
"He's so sweet.
Who wouldn't want a wonderful pet
like UGG Chomp?"

I looked at the photograph again.

I knew one thing.

Nobody would ever steal Lizzy's snake.

But I might find clues if I talked to
the party guests.

"I need to go inside and talk to your guests,"
I said.

I stepped toward the back door.

I noticed a thin layer of sugar on the ground.

It was everywhere.

Messy party, I thought.

I jumped over the sugar.

I was not going to be a messy detective.
The party guests were in the kitchen.
I saw Claude, Pip, and Oliver.
There was a table with a birthday cake,
cookies, chips, a nearly empty bowl of sugar,
and a large jug of water.
Claude was stirring a pitcher of lemonade.
Annie was playing with her dog, Fang.

Pip and Oliver were playing a board game.

"Hello," I said.

"I'm trying to find Lizzy's pet snake."

"We're *not* trying to find Lizzy's snake,"
Pip said. "As long as that monster is outside,
it's safe inside."

He pointed to a corner.

Rosamond's four cats were huddled together.

"Even *they* are afraid to be outside," he said.

"When was the last time anyone saw
UGG Chomp?" I asked.

"Right before the rain started," Annie said.
"He was in the back corner of the yard
hissing at Fang.
Fang was barking at him.
Then Fang lunged.
He knocked over a pitcher and spilled water
all over his new T-shirt."
"Fang's not wearing a T-shirt," I said.
"Rosamond took if off.
She put it in the dryer in the basement,"
Annie said.

"Then the rain started, and we
brought everything inside,"
Claude said.
"I brought in the sugar," Oliver said.
"Well, some of it.
I tripped on the top step
and dropped a pile of it on the porch.
I was the last person to come in."

Chapter Three

UGG Chomp! Where Are You?

There didn't seem to be any clues.
I would have to wait.
I would go outside.
I would listen for the sound
of someone screaming.
That would tell me where Lizzy's snake was.
But that would not be a good way
to solve the case.
I had to find UGG Chomp before
UGG Chomp found someone else.
Then I remembered Lizzy's car.

It was UGG Chomp's favorite place.
Maybe he'd gone looking for it.
I went out to the street.
There was no sign of Lizzy's car.
Lizzy's mother must have dropped her
and her snakes off at the party
and then driven away.
But UGG Chomp would not know
that the car was gone.
Maybe he'd come back to the street
to look for it.
Then what?

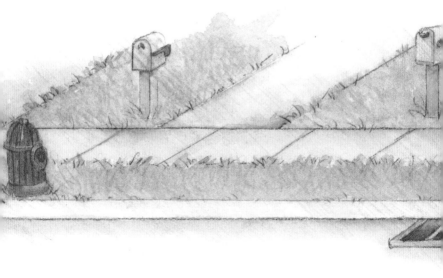

If he'd returned to the yard,
someone would have seen him.
If he'd slithered out onto the street,
we would have heard screaming
and police sirens by now.
I, Nate the Great,
decided that the street was
not the best place to look for clues.
I went back to the yard.
I walked over to the corner of the yard
where UGG Chomp had last been seen.

There were several large holes.

UGG Chomp had been busy.

Busy digging.

I, Nate the Great, knew one thing.

I was not going to look in any of the holes.

"Did you find him?" Lizzy asked.

"No," I said.

Lizzy noticed the holes too.

"He could be in any one of those," she said.

"UGG Chomp! Where are you?" she called.

I, Nate the Great, did not know
much about snakes.

But I knew that calling a snake's name
definitely would not work.

I walked around the yard.

Behind the yard was a large field
with tall grass.
It was the perfect place for a snake to hide.
"We need to search the field," I said.
"Snakes love tall grass."

Chapter Four
Snake Eyes

Sludge and I went out to the field.

The other party guests followed.

It was still raining.

The field was big.

The grass was tall.

The field was filled with buggy things with wings.

Flies, fleas, bees, mosquitoes, gnats, wasps, hornets, and a big flying thing that looked like a small bird.

I, Nate the Great,
was hoping that the big flying thing
that looked like a bird *was* a bird.
I also hoped we would find
UGG Chomp quickly.
We searched and searched.
We found many, many things.
Old toys, tires, books, candy wrappers,
and orange peels.
But we did not find UGG Chomp.
"Ouch!" Rosamond yelled. "I think
a mosquito bit me."

"I think I was bit by a flea," Pip said.

"I was just bit by something that looked
like a small bird," Oliver said.

"The only thing we've done out here
is feed the insects," I said.

Then Claude shouted from across the field.

"I did it! I solved the case!"

I ran to where I heard Claude's voice.

The other party guests followed me.

The insects followed the party guests.

Claude pointed to a swampy stream.
There were branches in the water.
There was also mud.
And leaves.
And hiding inside the leaves . . .
two shining eyes!

Chapter Five

How *Not* to Scare a Snake

"Claude, you did it!" Lizzy shouted.
"You're a detective.
You are Claude the Great."
"Not really," Claude said.
"I was looking for a dollar I'd lost.
I thought it fell into the water.
When I looked down,
I saw two eyes looking up at me."
Claude was always losing things.
But this time, he had found something.

He had found Lizzy's snake.

"The snake is buried under the leaves
and mud," I said. "We need to get it out."

"Maybe we could get him to come out if we
had some kind of bait," Annie said.

"Pancakes," I said.

"Snakes don't eat pancakes," Lizzy said.

"No," I said. "But I do.
They help me think.
It's hard to be a detective
when you're hungry."

"I have an idea," Annie said.
"I'll take Fang to the stream.
He'll bark at UGG Chomp
and scare him out of the water."

I turned to Lizzy.

"When was the last time
UGG Chomp ate?" I asked.

"Yesterday," she said.

"Ugg Chomp will be hungry," I said.
"Fang might become his lunch."
"Or snack," Lizzy said.
"UGG Chomp really loves to eat."

I walked toward the stream.
I looked at the water.
I saw two black eyes.

I saw fur.
I saw fur around
the two black eyes.

Then I saw two ears.
They were also covered in fur.

We had not found Lizzy's snake.
"I, Nate the Great, say that you are
not looking at a snake.
A snake would have scales around
its eyes. This animal has fur and ears."
"Snakes don't have fur or ears," Lizzy said.
"But beavers do," I said.
"We are looking at a beaver."

"So this is a dead end," Rosamond said.

"No it's not," Claude said.

"I just found my dollar in the mud!"

"We need to get back inside," I said.

"But how are we going to find my snake?"
Lizzy asked.

"He could be anywhere by now."

"Not anywhere," I said.

"He would go where a snake would go.

And we need to find out where that is.
We need to talk to someone who knows
about snakes."

"Who would that be?" Lizzy asked.

"A pet store, that's who.
Crazy Craig's Peculiar Pets.
They specialize in strange pets.
And they sell snakes.
I'll take Sludge with me."

Chapter Six
Call Me Crazy

Sludge and I walked in the rain
to Crazy Craig's Peculiar Pets.
I opened the front door.
I looked around.
I saw all sorts of peculiar pets.
Armadillos, skunks, hedgehogs, anteaters,
and, of course, snakes.
There were also many insects.
Including one that looked like a small bird.

Sludge whimpered and ran toward the door.

I followed him.

"Come on, Sludge," I said.

"We have a case to solve."

An odd-looking man walked over.

He was wearing a crazy T-shirt with

a picture of a snake with giant fangs.

He also had wild, crazy-looking hair.

Lots of wild, crazy-looking hair.

And a long beard.

We were in the right place.

"You must be Crazy Craig," I said.

"Yes," he said.

"But you can call me Crazy."

"I'd like to talk to you about snakes," I said.

"And I'd like to talk to *you* about snakes," Crazy Craig said.

"But I'd really like to talk to you about tarantulas!

We're having a huge sale on spiders!"

Sludge hid behind my legs.

"Maybe next time," I said.

"Right now I'm trying to find a missing ball python.

He vanished during a birthday party."

"Snakes disappear a lot," Crazy Craig said.

"Snakes have to keep their bodies warm. They'll look for rugs, blankets, and furnaces.

Any place that's warm."

"Thank you," I said.

"You've given us a good clue."

"Glad to help," Crazy Craig said.

"Now how about those tarantulas.

They make wonderful gifts."

He pointed to a large, hairy spider.

"His name is Alfred, and he's on sale.

If you buy him today,

I'll throw in his friend Henrietta."

I thought about Lizzy
and her strange snakes.
A tarantula might be
a good present for her.
But I, Nate the Great,
was on a case.

Chapter Seven

Snake in the Class

Sludge and I rushed back
to Rosamond's house.
It was pouring rain.
Everyone was inside.
"Snakes love warm places," I announced.
"We must find someplace warm."
I opened the back door
and looked at the yard.
I looked down at the porch.
The sugar was still there.

Then I remembered.
Oliver said that he had dropped
a *pile* of sugar on the porch.
But there was no pile.
Just a giant mess spread out
all over the place.
"Did anyone try to clean up
the pile of sugar?" I asked.
"No," Lizzy said.
"I, Nate the Great, say to all of you
that UGG Chomp has slithered his way
into the house."

"But we would have seen him,"
Claude said.
"Not if he slithered down
to the basement," I said.
"The basement has warm places
where a snake might go," Rosamond said.
"There's a furnace, a water heater,
blankets, and mattresses."
We all went down to the basement.
"Maybe you can sniff UGG Chomp out,"
I said to Sludge.
Sludge whimpered.

We searched the basement.
We looked under blankets.

We looked
in boxes.

We looked near
the furnace.
And the water heater.

Oliver picked up a corner of the rug.

"Not under here," he said.

"You didn't need to lift the rug," Lizzy said.

"If he were under it,
we would see a big bulge."

I, Nate the Great, knew that
UGG Chomp could not be in the basement.
He was too big to hide down here.
And yet, he *was* hiding.
We were playing hide-and-seek
with a giant snake.
The giant snake was winning.

"UGG Chomp must be really smart,"
I said.

"He's brilliant," Lizzy said.

"And he's never even gone to school."
I thought about UGG Chomp
in a classroom filled with children.

"Let me guess," I said.

"No school would take him."

"We tried them all," Lizzy said.

"Well, he's smart enough
to stay hidden," I said.

"And we're running out of places to look."

Then Sludge went to the dryer.
It was busy drying Fang's T-shirt.
"UGG Chomp is not in the dryer,"
Rosamond said.
"Why not?" Oliver asked.
"Snakes like heat. The dryer is hot."
"Because a snake can't open the dryer door,
let himself in, close the door,
and turn on the heat," Rosamond said.
"I didn't think about that," Oliver said.
"Neither did Sludge," Lizzy said.
"I guess he's not much of a detective."

Sludge growled.

"Sludge is a great detective," I said.

But Rosamond was right.

UGG Chomp could not have gotten inside the dryer on his own.

What was Sludge trying to tell me?

I looked at the dryer.

Then I walked around and looked behind it.

No snake.

Then I realized that Sludge had solved the case!

Chapter Eight
Hugs and Hisses

I went back up the basement stairs.
I walked through the kitchen and opened
the door to the backyard.
Sugar covered much of the porch.
But there was no sugar by the door.
UGG Chomp had never reached the door!
I looked to the side of the porch.
I saw a large bush next to the house.
Behind the bush, I heard a noise

coming from inside the house.
It was the sound of the dryer vent
blowing out hot air from the dryer
in the basement.
I, Nate the Great,
knew where UGG Chomp had gone.
I walked over and looked behind the bush.
There was UGG Chomp!
I looked at him.

He hissed at me.
The case was solved.
It was my job to find him.
It was not my job to move him.
A good detective knows his limits.
I went back inside the house.
"The case is solved," I said.
"Come here. I'll show you where
Ultra-Giant Goliath Chomp is."

Everyone followed me outside.

"You found him!" Lizzy exclaimed.

"My beautiful little baby!"

"Baby?" I said.

"Oh yes," Lizzy said.

"Someday he'll be twice as big as he is now."

"I can hardly wait," I said.

"Thank you so much, Nate the Great,"
Lizzy said.

"Don't thank me. Thank Sludge.

He solved the case."

"Well, thank you, Sludge," Lizzy said.

"Can you two stay for dinner?"

I looked at UGG Chomp.

He looked very hungry.

And he was smiling.

"I'd love to," I said. "But I have to get
back to Crazy Craig's before they close.
They're having a great sale on spiders."

~Extra~ Fun Activities!

What's Inside

Lizzy had snakes that were big, bigger, even bigger, and ultra-big. But not all snakes are big. Nate asked Crazy Craig about snakes of all kinds. This is what he learned.

NATE'S NOTES:
Big Snakes, Small Snakes,
Hard-to-Find Snakes

The smallest snakes in the world live on an island in the Caribbean Sea called Barbados. They are called threadsnakes. The first threadsnake was found in 2008. They may have been hard to find because they are just four inches long. That's about the size of a worm.

The heaviest snake in the world is the green anaconda. They can weigh up to 500 pounds. That's as heavy as twelve dogs! Sludge hopes that *isn't* true.

Another species of snake, a python, grew to be about 22 feet long. His name was Fluffy.

Mongooses are animals that eat snakes.
They look like ferrets.

Mongooses ate all the snakes on the island of Saint Lucia. The snakes were called Saint Lucia racers. Nobody saw a racer for almost forty years. Then one was found on a smaller island near Saint Lucia. The racers were safe on the small island. No mongooses live there. Racers are the rarest snake in the world. Only about eighteen survive today.

HOW TO MAKE SLIME

Snakes are actually not slimy. They are covered with dry scales, and sometimes they feel smooth. But it is fun to play with slime. You can make some at home.

Ask an adult to help you.

GET TOGETHER:

- a small bottle of white glue
- warm water
- a big spoon
- a small bottle of food coloring (any color)
- Borax*
- two bowls
- a tablespoon measure
- ½ cup measure

*Borax is a white powder like salt. You can buy it at the hardware store. It's not food, so don't eat it.

MAKE YOUR SLIME:

1. Empty the bottle of glue into one bowl.
2. Fill the empty bottle about halfway full with warm water. Swish it around.
3. Pour the water from the bottle into the bowl.
4. Add eight drops of food coloring. You can skip this step if you want.
5. Mix the water, glue, and food coloring together with the spoon.
6. Add 1 tablespoon of Borax into the second bowl. Add ½ cup of warm water. Stir slowly. The Borax should dissolve.
7. Slowly pour the Borax mixture into the glue mixture.
8. Stir as much as you can.
9. Pick up the slime. Some water may be left in the bowl.
10. Poke and squish the slime with your hands. It will get less sticky with time.

NATE'S NOTES:
Bugs That Bite

The field next to Rosamond's house was filled with buggy things with wings. How do bugs like mosquitoes find animals to bite? Nate went to the library to find out. This is what he learned.

Mosquitoes bite to eat, and the food they like is blood. They use the blood to feed their eggs.

Mosquitoes use smell to find people. They can smell you breathe from across a field. They can also smell sweat.

Mosquitoes can see people, too. It's easier for them to see people who are wearing dark colors.

Some people get bitten more than others.

Mosquitoes don't just bite people. They bite dogs and cats, too. They even bite snakes!

More than 80 different kinds of common bugs also bite people.

Funny Pages

Q: How do snakes sign their letters?
A: *With love and hisses.*

Q: What snake is a member of the band?
A: *The RATTLEsnake!*

Q: Why are snakes hard to fool?
A: *They don't have any legs to pull.*

Q: What do you call a python that everyone likes?
A: *A snake charmer.*

Q: What do snakes do after they fight?
A: *Hiss and make up.*

Q: What do you call a snake without clothes?
A: *Snaked!*

Q: Why couldn't the snake talk?
A: *He had a frog in his throat!*

A word about learning with

Nate The Great

The Nate the Great series is good fun and has been entertaining children for over forty years. These books are also valuable learning tools in and out of the classroom.

Nate's world—his home, his friends, his neighborhood—is one that every young person recognizes. Nate introduces beginning readers and those who have graduated to early chapter books to the detective mystery genre, and they respond to Nate's commitment to solving the case and helping his friends.

What's more, as Nate the Great solves his cases, readers learn with him. Nate unravels mysteries by using evidence collection, cogent reasoning, problem-solving, analytical skills, and logic in a way that teaches readers to develop critical-thinking abilities. The stories help children start discussions about how to approach difficult situations and give them tools to resolve them.

When you read a Nate the Great book with a child, or when a child reads a Nate the Great mystery on his or her own, the child is guaranteed a satisfying ending that will have taught him or her important classroom and life skills. We know that you and your children will enjoy reading and learning from Nate the Great's wonderful stories as much as we do.

Find out more at NatetheGreatBooks.com.

Happy reading and learning with Nate!

Solve all the mysteries with

Nate the Great

- ❑ Nate the Great and the Crunchy Christmas
- ❑ Nate the Great Saves the King of Sweden
- ❑ Nate the Great and Me: The Case of the Fleeing Fang
- ❑ Nate the Great and the Monster Mess
- ❑ Nate the Great, San Francisco Detective
- ❑ Nate the Great and the Big Sniff
- ❑ Nate the Great on the Owl Express
- ❑ Nate the Great Talks Turkey
- ❑ Nate the Great and the Hungry Book Club
- ❑ Nate the Great, Where Are You?
- ❑ Nate the Great and the Missing Birthday Snake
- ❑ Nate the Great and the Wandering Word

MARJORIE WEINMAN SHARMAT has written more than 130 books for children and young adults, as well as movie and TV novelizations. Her books have been translated into twenty-four languages. The award-winning Nate the Great series, hailed in *Booklist* as "groundbreaking," has resulted in Nate's real-world appearances in many *New York Times* crossword puzzles, sporting a milk mustache in magazines and posters, residing on more than 28 million boxes of Cheerios, and touring the country in musical theater. Marjorie Weinman Sharmat and her husband, Mitchell Sharmat, have also coauthored many books, including titles in both the Nate the Great and the Olivia Sharp series.

ANDREW SHARMAT is the son of Marjorie Weinman Sharmat and Mitchell Sharmat. *Nate the Great and the Missing Birthday Snake* is his first collaboration with his mother.

JODY WHEELER developed a greater-than-average interest in children's books at an early age, having been influenced and encouraged by her great-aunt Opal Wheeler, a prolific writer of books for young readers in the 1950s. Since being trained as a fine artist and educator, Jody has enjoyed working on projects ranging from picture books to educational texts and magazines, and from greeting cards to coloring books. Jody Wheeler divides her time between Manhattan and Ballston Spa, New York.